THIS BOOK BELONGS TO

....

....

All *Hey Duggee*
books are printed on
paper from responsibly
managed sources.
This *Hey Duggee*
book is printed with
environmentally friendly
vegetable inks.

LADYBIRD BOOKS

UK | USA | Canada | Ireland | Australia | India | New Zealand | South Africa

Ladybird Books is part of the Penguin Random House group of companies
whose addresses can be found at global.penguinrandomhouse.com.

www.penguin.co.uk   www.puffin.co.uk   www.ladybird.co.uk

 Penguin
Random House
UK

First published 2023
001

Text and illustrations copyright © Studio AKA Limited, 2023
Adapted by Sarah Delmege, based on "Loving the Green Planet Badge"
written by Will Maclean

Printed in Italy

The authorized representative in the EEA is Penguin Random House Ireland,
Morrison Chambers, 32 Nassau Street, Dublin D02 YH68

A CIP catalogue record for this book is available from the British Library

ISBN: 978-0-241-60923-1

All correspondence to:
Ladybird Books, Penguin Random House Children's
One Embassy Gardens, 8 Viaduct Gardens, London SW11 7BW

HEY DUGGEE

THE GREEN PLANET BADGE

NORRIE   TAG   DUGGEE   BETTY   ROLY   HAPPY

It's a lovely summer's day,
and the Squirrels have found
the perfect tree to run round.

When the Squirrels stop for a glass of juice,
Duggee gives the tree trunk a friendly pat.
"Ah-woof!" says Duggee. Trees are amazing.

Duggee tells the
Squirrels that trees
like this one are
some of the most
important living
things on Earth.

The Squirrels don't understand. How could a tree be so important?

IT'S NOT ALIVE!

IT'S JUST WOOD!

"Woof woof!" says Duggee. This tree is very much alive, Squirrels!

In fact, the biggest
living thing on
Earth is a tree –
the mighty sequoia.

"But why are trees so important?" asks Norrie.
Duggee can explain. He has his **Green Planet Badge!**

AH-WOOF!

Duggee and the Squirrels go to the clubhouse.

"Ah-woof woof, woof woof," says Duggee.

It all starts with the sun.

"The sun?" asks Betty.

"Ah-woof!" says Duggee.

The sun shines on to the trees' leaves.

"Wow!" gasps Betty. "There are so many leaves."

There are . . .

green ones,

yellow ones,

big ones

and small ones!

It's a good thing
there are so many,
because leaves are
very important.

Leaves catch the sunlight, which helps them make food for the tree to grow . . .

AAAAAH!

and they make air for everyone to breathe.

SIGH!

Leaves are pretty
important, aren't they?

AH-WOOF!

Norrie spots something on the tree trunk . . . lots of little things!

WHAT ARE THOSE?

"Woof woof!" says Duggee. They are insects.

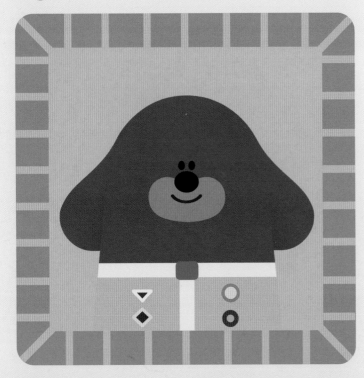

"What are they doing?" asks Betty. Some of them have been collecting leaves from the top of the tree, and some of them live up there.

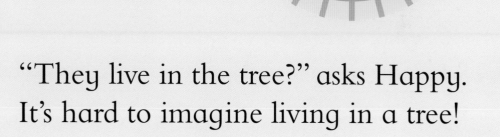

"They live in the tree?" asks Happy. It's hard to imagine living in a tree!

"Woof woof,"
says Duggee. Lots of
animals live in trees.

Trees are home to spiders . . .

bats . . .

and all sorts of birds.

WAAAAAH!

Sometimes, birds stay in the same tree . . .

all their lives.

"Ah-woof woof!" says Duggee.
Trees and plants are the basis
of all life on Earth.
"Oooh!" gasp the Squirrels.

The Squirrels follow Duggee outside to the garden. There are so many plants and animals living there!

Tag chases a butterfly.

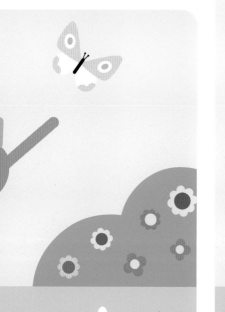

Roly stares up at a very tall sunflower.

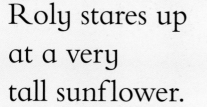

All the fruit
and vegetables
we grow come
from trees
and plants.

PLOP!

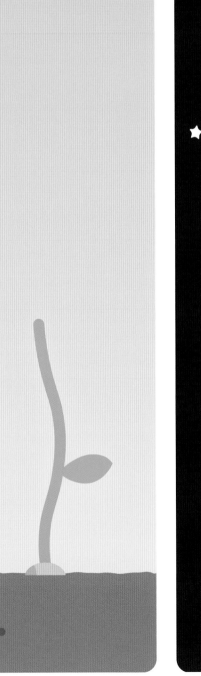

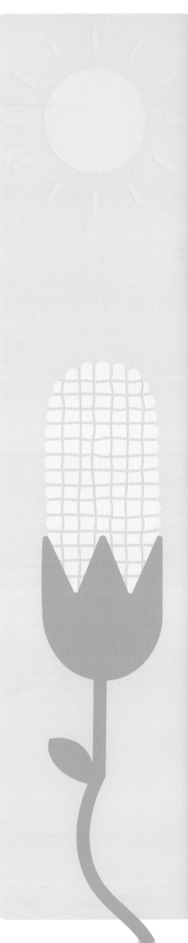

We depend on plants for every mouthful of food we eat ...

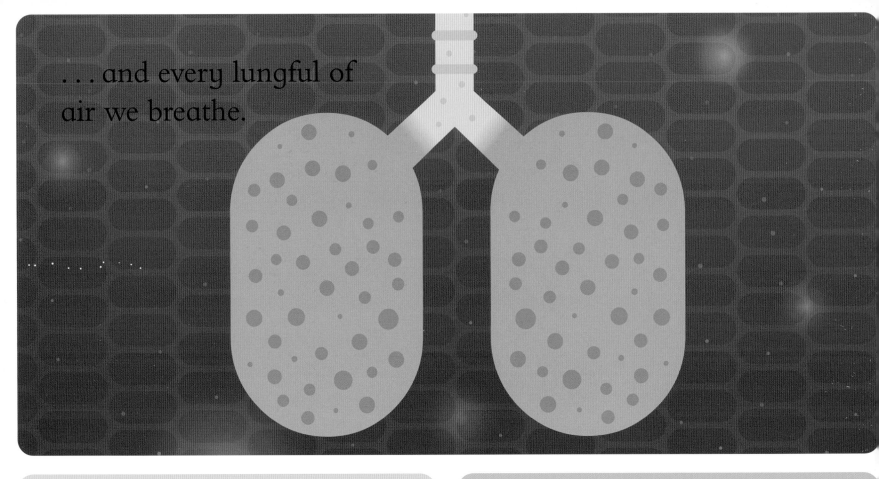

. . . and every lungful of air we breathe.

Duggee takes a deep breath of air in . . .

1. . . 2 . . . 3 . . .

The Squirrels practise breathing in . . .

and out . . .

"Ah-woof!" says Duggee. And that's why trees are so important!

We must take care of our plants . . .

and our planet.

The Squirrels have learned
so much today!

It's getting late, and
the Squirrels are tired.

Haven't the Squirrels done well today, Duggee?
They have definitely earned their **Green Planet Badges**.

Now there's just time
for one last thing
before the Squirrels
go home . . .

"TREE HUG!"